Dilly
the
Dinosaur

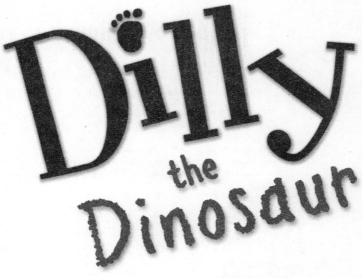

the
Dinosaur

Tony Bradman
Illustrated by Susan Hellard

EGMONT

We bring stories to life

First published in Great Britain 1986
by Piccadilly Press Ltd
Published 1987 by Egmont UK Ltd
239 Kensington High Street, London W8 6SA.

40 39 38 37 36

ISBN 978 0 7497 4682 7

A CIP catalogue record for this title is available from the British Library

Printed and bound in Great Britain by the CPI Group

30602/14

EGMONT LUCKY COIN

Our story began over a century ago, when seventeen-year-old Egmont Harald Petersen found a coin in the street.

He was on his way to buy a flyswatter, a small hand-operated printing machine that he then set up in his tiny apartment.

The coin brought him such good luck that today Egmont has offices in over 30 countries around the world. And that lucky coin is still kept at the company's head offices in Denmark.

Contents

1 Dirty Dilly

There are four of us in my family.

First of all, there's my mother and my father. And there's me, of course. I'm their oldest child, their daughter. My name is Dorla. That makes three, doesn't it?

And then, last but certainly not least, there's Dilly, my little brother.

1

I suppose I shouldn't say so, but when Dilly was a baby I didn't like him very much. Once, not long after he was born, I even asked Mother to take him back to the hospital where she got him. Well, he did cry a lot, after all.

I love Dilly now though, I really do. He doesn't cry like a baby any more, although he can make plenty of noise when he feels like it. He can be a lot of fun, too, but sometimes he can be a real problem, as you'll see.

Part of the trouble is that Dilly can be very, very stubborn. When he decides to do something, it's hard to get him to change his mind.

For instance, Dilly used to like water more than anything else in the whole world. He loved to play pouring-out games, and splashing games, and getting-as-wet-as-you-can games all the time. In fact, Father said that Dilly liked water a little *too* much.

"Every time he has a bath," said Father, "I finish up wetter than him!"

But Mother and I were sure that Father enjoyed those getting-wet games as much as Dilly—even though he wouldn't admit it.

Then just the other morning, when he got up, Dilly decided that he didn't like water after all. He told Mother that he didn't want to brush his teeth, or wash, or have a bath, or play with water.

Mother was confused.

"That's strange, Dilly," she said. "I thought water was your favourite thing. Why don't you like it any more?"

Dilly looked very stubborn.

"I just don't, that's all," he said.

"But Dilly," said Mother, "you'll get very dirty if you don't wash. Very dirty, and very smelly."

"I don't care," said Dilly, with his nose in the air. "I like dirt. I like dirt a lot." Dilly smiled. "In fact, dirt is now my favourite thing. And I don't care if I smell."

4

Mother looked hard at Dilly.

"Okay," she said at last. "Have it your way."

All that day, it seemed as if Dilly went out of his way to play the dirtiest games he could think of. He rolled in the dirt a lot, and by the evening he looked very grubby indeed.

Mother thought that Dilly would have forgotten all about not liking water by the time it came to having a bath before bed. So she was smiling when she called him in. She wasn't smiling for long, though.

"Come on, Dilly," she said. "Your bath is ready."

Dilly didn't stop rolling in the dirt.

"I'm not having a bath," he said. "I don't like water, remember?"

Now I could see from Mother's face that she was a little cross.

"Dilly Dinosaur," she said, "I think it's time we forgot all about this not washing business. You have got to have a bath. You can't possibly go to bed in that state."

"But I don't want a bath," said Dilly. "I don't like water any more."

"Dilly Dinosaur! Now you'll stop all this nonsense, come indoors and get in that tub!"

Dilly didn't say anything for a moment. But I could tell from looking at his stubborn face what was coming next. He opened his mouth and let loose with his ultra-special, 150-mile-per-hour super-scream, the one that makes Mother wince, Father clap in his earplugs, and me hide under the bed.

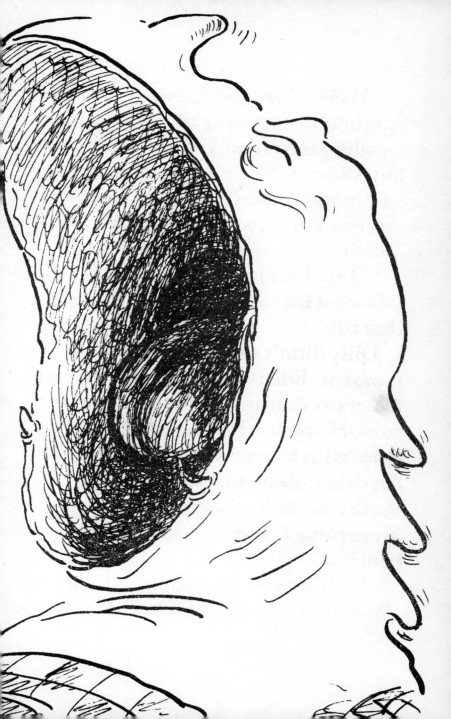

When Dilly had finished, Mother and Father whispered to each other for a while. Afterwards they told me that they had decided to let Dilly find out for himself what it really meant not to wash, or have a bath, or brush your teeth.

"Okay, Dilly," said Mother at the time. "Have it your way. Go to bed dirty."

And that's exactly what Dilly did.

Dilly didn't wash or brush his teeth the next morning, either. He just got dirtier, and dirtier, and dirtier. He played in the dirt all day, and in the evening, Father called him in.

"Now, Dilly," said Father. "Are you going to have a bath tonight or not?"

Dilly looked disgusting. There was food all round his mouth and down his

front, and his teeth looked dreadful.
But he still didn't want to have a bath.
He looked at Father, and then opened
his mouth the way he did when he was
winding up to let loose an ultra-
special, 150-mile-per-hour super-
scream . . .

"Okay, okay, Dilly," said Father.
"Have it your way. No bath again
tonight. But you'll be sorry!"

Dilly just smiled.

The next day, Dilly's best friend
Dixie was coming to play. She lives
right next door, and Dilly just loves to
play with her. Usually they play with
water a lot, because Dixie loves water
as much as Dilly does—or at least, as
much as Dilly used to. She loves
pouring-out games, and splashing
games, and all those getting-as-wet-
as-you-can games.

But that day, Dilly didn't want to play with water. He wanted Dixie to play his new favourite game—rolling in the dirt.

Dixie didn't want to. In fact, Dixie looked really disappointed when Dilly said he didn't want to play any water games.

After a while, too, Dixie began to look at Dilly in a strange way. She looked, and she looked, and she looked. And she sniffed, too.

"Dilly," she said, "you look very funny. You're all dirty."

Dilly smiled proudly.

"That's because I don't like water any more," he said. "I don't play with water, and I don't wash, or brush my teeth or have baths."

Dixie didn't smile.
"Dilly, you're smelly, too," she

said. "You're a smelly Dilly, and I don't want to play with you today."

Dilly stopped smiling.

Not long after, Dixie said she wanted to go home. Dilly didn't say anything. But I could see that he had his thoughtful look on his face.

That evening, Mother called Dilly in. She didn't say anything about baths, or dirt, or washing. It was Dilly himself who brought up the subject.

"About water," he said, all of a sudden.

"Yes, Dilly?" said Mother.

"I think it's all right. I've decided I like it again."

He had, too. And he had that really stubborn look on his face, as well.

"Oh really?" was all that Mother said.

"In fact, water is my favourite

thing," said Dilly. "Could I have a bath—*right now*?"

Mother looked at him very hard for a moment, trying hard not to smile.

"Okay, Dilly," she said at last. "Have it your way."

2 Dilly's Birthday Disaster

I love birthdays, don't you? It's great to have presents and birthday cards, a cake with candles and everybody singing "Happy birthday to you" at the tops of their voices. In fact, apart from Christmas, my birthday is my favourite day of the whole year.

Dilly loves birthdays too. At least, he loves it when it's *his* birthday. He talks about it all year round. Why, he starts asking Mother and Father when

14

his next birthday is as soon as his birthday is over! Only the other day he was pestering Father to show him on the calendar which day was his birthday.

"Is it on that day?" he asked, pointing to the calendar.

"No, Dilly, your birthday's not for months yet." Father turned the pages of the calendar until he came to the right month. He showed Dilly the day. Dilly looked very closely at where Father was pointing.

"Is that tomorrow?" he said.

"No, Dilly," said Father. "I've already told you, your birthday isn't for a long time yet."

Dilly kept his eyes on the calendar. He had his very thoughtful look on his face, too. After a while, he said:

"So is my birthday . . . next week?"

15

Father sighed.

"No, Dilly, it's not next week," he said. "It's not for ages yet."

"So when *is* my birthday then?" said Dilly. He was beginning to look a little cross—and so was Father.

"Don't worry about it, Dilly," he said. "You'll know when it's your birthday all right."

Mother laughed. "I'm sure we all will," she said.

But Dilly didn't laugh. He looked very cross indeed, and he stomped off to play. Later I could hear him talking to himself. I couldn't be sure, but it

sounded as if he were singing, "Happy birthday . . . to me".

Father said that Dilly didn't really understand about time yet, and that he would probably forget about his birthday after a while.

But Dilly didn't forget.

I'm sure he would have forgotten if something else hadn't happened to remind him. For a few days later I woke up, and it was my favourite day of the whole year—*my* birthday!

I had lots of terrific presents. And I had so many birthday cards that there was hardly room on the shelf to stand them all up!

One of those cards was from Dilly. He had made it himself, with a little help from Mother. Dilly had given it to me and wished me a happy birthday. But I could see from his face that he

wasn't very happy. I had a good idea
why he wasn't happy, too.

Anyway, I was very excited because
I was going to have a birthday party.
All my friends were coming, and
Father was making me a birthday
cake. I helped him make the mixture.
It was a chocolate cake, and it looked
delicious.

"Hey, Dilly," Father said after he'd

let me lick the mixing spoon, "Dilly, do you want to try some of your sister's cake?"

Dilly didn't say anything. He just looked very cross and stomped off to his room.

"Oh well," said Father as he put the cake in to bake, "perhaps Dilly will be happier when it's party time."

I didn't think he would, though.

Later on, Mother and I started blowing up the balloons ready for the party. Then there was a stomp, stomp, stomp, the door crashed open, and Dilly was standing in front of us.

Mother stopped blowing into her balloon.

"My, my, Dilly," she said. "What an entrance! And what can we do for you?"

"Is it my birthday today too?" he asked. He had a very cross look on his face.

"No, Dilly," said Mother. "Your

birthday's not for ages yet. It's your
sister's birthday today. But that
doesn't mean you can't enjoy it too.
Why don't you help us blow up some
balloons? You like balloons.''

"I don't,'' he said. ''I hate stupid
balloons. And why isn't it my birthday
today? I want it to be my birthday!''

"You only get one birthday a year,''
said Mother, ''and I'm afraid yours is
still to come.'' Then Mother smiled.
"Why don't you look on the bright
side, Dilly? You can enjoy your sister's
birthday party today and still look

21

forward to your own."

Dilly didn't smile.

"But I want it to be my birthday *today*," shouted Dilly, and he stamped his foot. Now I know there's one thing that Mother can't bear, and it's to see Dilly stamping his foot and hear him shouting like that. She looked as cross as Dilly!

"Dilly, you are a very bad dinosaur," she said in her sternest voice. "It isn't your birthday today, it's your sister's, and that's all there is to it. And if you don't behave like a good dinosaur, then you won't be having a birthday at all this year."

Just at that moment, Father came through the door. He was carrying my birthday cake on a plate.

"Hurrah!" he said. "Look what I've got!"

Dilly looked up at Father. And then he said: "It's not fair!", and let loose with his ultra-special, 150-mile-per-hour super-scream, the one that makes Mother cover her head with a cushion, me hide behind the sofa . . . and Father drop delicious chocolate birthday cakes right on the floor, where they smash into a thousand messy pieces!

Father was cross, Mother was cross—and I cried and cried and cried. My beautiful birthday cake was all over the carpet!

Mother marched Dilly out of the room. He was crying too, now. I heard her telling him off.

"Dilly Dinosaur," she said, "you will go to your bedroom and stay there until you're ready to say sorry and be nice to Dorla on her birthday."

Dilly didn't say anything. All I heard was him stomping off to his room, stomp, stomp, stomp—and SLAM! went his door.

"And don't slam your door!" shouted Mother. But there was no reply.

Dilly didn't come out for his morning drink of juice. He didn't come out for his lunch, either. And he didn't come out when my friends started to arrive for the party.

But then you know that Dilly can be very stubborn.

I didn't like the idea of Dilly sitting in his room all alone on my birthday, though. So I went up and knocked on his door.

"Come on, Dilly," I said. "Come out and say sorry, and then you can join in the fun."

I listened at the door, but there was no answer. I did hear something, though. It sounded like Dilly sniffing—but I couldn't be sure.

Anyway, we had so much fun at my party that I didn't have time to think about Dilly. We played all sorts of games, we ran, we jumped, and we shouted, and Mother and Father didn't tell any of us off *once*.

But I still didn't have a birthday cake, and that made me feel a little sad.

Then just as everybody was getting

ready to go, I heard a noise coming from the kitchen. Father heard it too.

"What's that noise?" he said.

And then there was a much bigger noise.

CRASH!

It sounded like a pile of plates falling out of a cupboard and smashing on the floor. And that's exactly what it was. For when we opened the door and looked in the kitchen, we saw . . . guess who? Dilly Dinosaur, and he was sitting in the middle of the floor surrounded by broken plates, holding a bowl.

Well . . . none of us knew what to say. None of us, that is, except Dilly.

"I'm sorry," he said, and gave us his biggest and best don't-tell-me-off-yet-I've-got-an-excuse smile. "I thought I'd make you another birthday cake,"

he said, "to make up for the one Father dropped." And Dilly showed us what he had in the bowl. It looked like a mess of broken eggs and flour and cocoa. There was more of the same mess on the table and all over the floor.

"But Dilly," said Mother, "how did you break all those plates?"

"I was trying to get a pretty plate out of the cupboard," he said, "to put the cake on. But it was on the bottom of all the other plates. So I had to pull, and pull, and pull, and . . ."

"Don't tell me," said Mother. "I know the rest."

Dilly was in a lot of trouble. Mother and Father were rather cross with him, even though he had said sorry for being bad. They did tell him off, but not too much. They said that he was very bad to make such a mess in the kitchen and to break the plates, but that he was also good for trying to make up for the spoiled cake.

Which all left Dilly feeling a little confused.

"So am I a bad dinosaur or not?" he asked.

Mother and Father laughed.

"You're not too bad, Dilly. Not too bad at all," said Father. "And now it's time for bed."

And do you know what Dilly said then?

"Is it my birthday tomorrow?"

Father sighed.

"Dilly . . ." he said, "to bed!"

3 Dilly's Rainy Day

When I got up this morning, I looked
out of the window. I was hoping it
would be a nice, sunny day. But it
wasn't, it was raining. Actually, it
wasn't just raining, it was pouring
down.

At breakfast, Dilly looked really fed
up.

"What's wrong, Dilly?" asked
Father. "Don't you like your cereal?"

"I don't like the rain," said Dilly.

"But Dilly," said Father, "we need the rain. If it didn't rain, nothing would grow, and we wouldn't have trees to look at or flowers to smell or any food to eat."

"I don't like the rain," said Dilly again, in a very grumpy way.

"And why is that?" asked Mother.

"Because when it rains like this I have to stay indoors, and I get bored when I stay indoors."

Now if there's one thing we all worry about, it's Dilly getting *bored*. For when Dilly gets bored, he usually ends up being bad. In fact, when he's bored, Dilly is as bad as he can possibly be. And as you know by now, that can be really pretty bad indeed.

So Mother and Father and I were all a bit worried, to say the least.

"Ah . . . well . . . okay . . . right,"

said Mother. "I think I'll find those old puzzles of your sister's I promised I'd dig out. And what else can we find to keep you amused?"

"It's all right," said Dilly. "I think I'll just go to my room."

"Never mind, Dilly," said Father. "It will probably rain cats and dogs this morning, and then the sun will shine this afternoon and you can play outside."

Dilly stopped and looked at Father. "Will it really?" he said.

"I'm sure it will," said Father.

Dilly looked at Father in a very strange way. Then he went off to his room. But I could see that he wasn't looking quite so fed up any more. He even seemed to be quite happy, almost as if he were looking forward to something.

A little while later, Mother found the puzzles and games she had been looking for. She went to Dilly's room and asked him if he wanted to play with them. At first he didn't hear her. He was staring out of the window at the rain.

"Dilly, do you want these games or not?"

"No, Mother."

" 'No thank you, Mother', is what you should say, Dilly," she said, without thinking. Usually Dilly gets his stubborn face, and starts to act up when he's corrected. But all he said was: "Sorry, Mother," and kept looking out at the rain. Mother was really surprised that Dilly was being so well-behaved. So was I, I can tell you!

"Oh, okay, Dilly. I'll just leave them here for you. Perhaps you could play with them later." Mother put the games down. "Perhaps your sister will show you how to play with them, too," she said. "Be a good girl and help us keep Dilly happy," she whispered in my ear.

I tried, but Dilly didn't seem to need my help. I said he could play with any of my toys, even my best birthday doll, but he just kept looking out of the window at the rain. I said he could play with my painting set if he wanted to. I hide it on my top shelf so that he can't get it.

But Dilly just stared out of the window.

Later on, Father took him his morning drink of juice and asked him

if he'd like to watch TV.

"No thank you, Father," said Dilly.

Now that was really not like Dilly at all. Usually he would have grabbed his drink, spilled it down his front, and crashed out of the door to watch the TV. Father looked a little worried. He felt Dilly's forehead.

"You haven't got a temperature,"

he said. "And you don't look ill. Are you sure you're feeling all right?"

"Yes thank you, Father," said Dilly, who took a sip of his drink—and kept staring out of the window at the rain. Father just shook his head as if he didn't understand.

Dilly stayed in his room all that morning. He didn't do anything, but he didn't look bored, and he certainly didn't do anything bad.

"Do you know," said Mother, "I think this is the longest time that Dilly has ever behaved himself."

"Yes," said Father. "I wonder whatever could be the matter?"

A little later, it was lunchtime.

"Come on, Dilly," Mother called. "Your lunch is ready."

But Dilly didn't come down.

"Dilly!" shouted Mother.

But still Dilly didn't come down.
Father said he would go up to get him.

"Come on, Dilly," he said, "don't
you want your lunch? It's your
favourite."

"No thank you, Father," said Dilly,
without looking round, "I don't want
any lunch today."

I looked at Father. He seemed a
little cross.

"Dilly, you must have your lunch.
Now come on, and be quick about it."

I looked at Dilly. And yes, he had that stubborn look on his face. I thought, here we go, any second he's going to let loose with his ultra-special, 150-mile-per-hour super-scream, the one that makes Mother go pale, Father hide in the cellar and me sit with my coat over my head.

But he didn't. All he said was: "Okay, Father," and he came down, as meek as meek could be. He ate all his lunch and didn't complain once, and then he went straight back to his room to look at the rain from his window again.

Mother and Father were really confused by now, and so was I. Why was Dilly behaving so well? What could possibly be wrong with him? It

was all a great puzzle.

"Shall I call the doctor?" said Mother.

"I don't know," said Father. "Dilly bit the doctor the last time we called him out, remember?" And he had. When the doctor had tried to take Dilly's temperature he had screamed and bitten him really hard on the finger. There was even some blood, and the doctor said he was never coming back to our house.

A little later, Dilly came out of his room.

"Father," he said.

"Yes, Dilly?" said Father.

"I've been looking out of my window at the rain," said Dilly.

"I know," said Father.

"It's been raining all day," said Dilly.

"I know," said Father.

"It's still raining," said Dilly.

"I know," said Father.

Dilly looked at Father in a strange way.

"Well, when are the cats and dogs going to come?" he said. "I've been waiting all day for it to rain cats and dogs like you said."

Now you know, and I know, and Mother and Father knew, that it doesn't really rain cats and dogs. It's just a saying that means it's raining very hard.

But Dilly didn't know that, and now we knew why he had been behaving so well all day, and why he had been staring out of the window at the rain. He was waiting for *real* cats and dogs to fall out of the sky like rain!

Father laughed, and so did Mother.

"Oh, Dilly," they said, "it doesn't really rain cats and dogs!"

But Dilly didn't laugh. In fact, Dilly

looked very cross indeed.

"But I want it to rain cats and dogs," he shouted. And then he stamped his foot, and then . . . he let loose with his you-know-what, his ultra-special, 150-mile-per-hour super-scream.

And do you know, Mother and Father looked quite pleased when they heard it. That evening Dilly made up for being well-behaved by being as bad as he could be. Still, at least we were used to him being that way!

The next morning, something funny happened, too. Dilly woke us all up very early. He was terribly excited about something he'd seen from his window. He led us into his room to show us.

We all looked out. On the windowsill a tabby cat was sitting, cleaning her paws.

"See," said Dilly, "it did rain cats
and dogs last night after all."
Father laughed.
"Well, it must have rained cats, at
least."
And Dilly smiled.

4 Dilly Does Some Painting

Dilly can be good sometimes, and Dilly can be bad, as you know by now. In fact, you've seen Dilly being very bad, haven't you? But there was one day when Dilly was more badly behaved than he had ever been before.

It was the day when Mother and Father decided to start decorating their bedroom.

"What does deco . . . deco . . . what does that word mean?" asked Dilly.

"It means that Mother and Father are going to paint the walls, silly Dilly," I said.

"Now don't be like that, Dorla," said Father. "We haven't done any decorating for a long time, so Dilly can't be expected to know what it means."

I could see that Dilly had his thoughtful look on his face.

"I like painting," he said. "Can I do some painting, too?"

Father smiled.

"I'm sure you can do some painting, Dilly," he said. "But you have to remember it's not like the painting you usually do."

"No," said Mother. "We're not painting pictures, like you do, we're going to paint all the walls the same colour."

"That sounds very boring," said Dilly.

Mother and Father laughed.

"It might be boring to you," said Father, "but it's the way we want it. Anyway, you two dinosaurs can help us get everything ready to start with."

It was all very exciting. We had to take the bed and the big wardrobe out of the bedroom, and then we put big sheets all over the carpet so that the paint wouldn't drip on it. I helped, but Dilly really only got in the way. Father kept shouting at him.

"Watch out, there, Dilly," he shouted. "This wardrobe is heavy! Don't get under my feet like that, you'll get hurt!"

Then Mother and Father got out the ladders and the paint and the brushes. And that's when Dilly started

46

to bounce up and down with
excitement.

"Oooh," he said, "I want to use that
big brush! Can I? Can I please? Can I
please please please?"

"I'm afraid you can't, Dilly," said
Mother. "I think it's a little too big for
you."

47

"But I want the big brush," said Dilly. I looked at his face, and I could see that he was looking very stubborn.

Mother looked quite stubborn, too.

"Dilly Dinosaur," she said, "if you want to do some painting, you will use *this* brush and no other!" And she held up a much smaller brush in front of him.

I thought for a moment that Dilly was going to let loose a 150-mile-per-hour ultra-special super-scream—but he didn't. I think that he wanted to do some painting much, much more than he wanted to be bad.

Mother gave me a brush, and we all started painting the walls.

It really was a lot of fun, and we seemed to be getting on very well at first. Mother and Father asked me to keep an eye on Dilly, though, just to make sure that he didn't get in too much of a mess.

But I forgot to watch him because I was enjoying myself so much. And the next thing I knew was that my feet felt all wet and sticky.

Dilly had knocked the paint pot over and was stomping in the paint, stomp, stomp, stomp! He was making such a mess.

Well, Mother and Father told him off, of course, and then they had to take his clothes off and get him cleaned up. I had to wash all the paint off my feet, too. Mother and Father were very, very cross, and they said Dilly had to stay in his room for the rest of the day.

Later I was told to check up on Dilly.

I took a deep breath and opened Dilly's door.

"Hello, Dorla," said Dilly.

He looked very strange. In fact, he looked very strange indeed. I couldn't believe what I was seeing.

Dilly was completely covered in paint, from head to foot. In his hand there was a paintbrush, and paint was dripping off the end of it on to his bedroom floor. But it was worse than that.

I looked round, and saw that the room was in a real mess. Dilly had moved his bed away from the wall a little, and pulled all the drawers out of his bedside cabinet. He had pulled all the books off his shelf, and piled them in the middle of the floor.

And he had done something else which was very bad indeed.

Dilly had painted on the wall. There was a great big splodge of different colours on the wall next to his wardrobe, and there was green paint all over the carpet by the door.

"I've been doing some painting," he said. "I climbed up and got your painting set down from your top shelf," he said. "I tried to move my bed, but it was too heavy. The wall looks pretty, doesn't it? Do you like it?"

Dilly was smiling.

Anyway, I went to get Mother and Father. When they saw what Dilly had done they didn't know what to say.

After that they were very angry and told Dilly off. Dilly cried, and Mother and Father made him help with the clearing up, which took ages. That just made him look fed up.

"Now, Dilly," said Father, "you're going to have to have a long bath to get all that paint off."

Dilly looked even more fed up.

"But I don't want a bath. I've decided that I don't like water again."

Father looked very cross indeed.

"Dilly Dinosaur," he said, "you're not going to start all that nonsense about not liking water again, are you?"

I looked at Dilly. He did have that stubborn look on his face, and for a second I thought he was going to let loose an ultra-special, 150-mile-per-hour super-scream . . . but he didn't.

"Okay, Father," he said. "Have it your way."

And Mother and Father just smiled.

That evening, when Dilly was in bed, he said that from now on he wouldn't be a bad dinosaur any more. In fact, he said that from now on he was going to be the best-behaved dinosaur in the whole wide world.

But I'm not sure whether Dilly can be the best-behaved dinosaur in the world.

Do you think he can?

EGMONT

If you thought this *book* was brilliant, that's probably because it was! But there's loads more fun still to be had - welcome to the wonderworld of . . .

Jelly Pie

It's home to the funniest reads around.

AGATHA PARROT

WAHOO! I'm Agatha Parrot. Read my book to find out all about the time Miss Barking tried to chop off my friend Martha's head with a cardboard axe, but instead it floated off and exploded ha ha brilliant!

Funniness rating:
Total Chaos factor: 5 out of 5 octopus pizzas

YOU'RE A BAD MAN, MR GUM!

Good evening. Mr Gum is a complete horror who hates children, animals, fun and corn on the cob. This book's all about him. And an angry fairy who lives in his bathtub. And Jake the dog, and a little girl called Polly and an evil butcher. And there's heroes and sweets and adventures and EVERYTHING.

Funniness rating:
Barking Mad factor: 5 out of 5 bags of sticks

SPUD GOES GREEN

Hello! My name's Spud and I have decided to go green . . . No, I don't mean TURN green, I mean go green, by looking after the planet sort of thing. Don't be a meanie . . . become a GREENIE!

Funniness rating: 🍬🍬🍬🍬🍬
Save the Environment factor: 5 out of 5 beetles

ELLIE MAY WOULD LIKE TO BE TAKEN SERIOUSLY FOR A CHANGE

Dear Everybody,
I'm an incredibly famous film star! I get to sign autographs and be in magazines and I have my very own Jeffrey to look after me! Hooray! But I'm also a very serious person. I love nature. I have a bag decorated with butterflies. And that's why I'm going to save a nature reserve. It can't be that hard . . . can it?
Love, Ellie May.

Funniness rating: 🍬🍬🍬🍬🍬
Amazingly Amazingness factor: 5 out of 5 fudge cakes

I AM NOT A LOSER

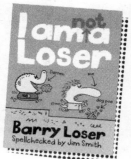

My name is Barry Loser, and I've never minded that being my name because my coolness has always cancelled it out, but ever since Darren Darrenofski joined school with his horrible little crocodile face he's been completely ruining my life about it.

Funniness rating:
Keelness factor: 5 out of 5 ringpulls

ALIEN IN MY BELLYBUTTON

I was in for a shock when I crash landed my spaceship in Pete Perkins' belly button. Flampering pufflefarts, he was huge! But now we've teamed up for a very important and very disgusting reason. Join us on our mission. You'll encounter a cheese-powered jetpack, a stinky grandpa and a whole load of trouble!

Funniness rating:
Grot factor: 5 out of 5 toe-cheese chimples

EGMONT PRESS: ETHICAL PUBLISHING

Egmont Press is about turning writers into successful authors and children into passionate readers – producing books that enrich and entertain. As a responsible children's publisher, we go even further, considering the world in which our consumers are growing up.

Safety First
Naturally, all of our books meet legal safety requirements. But we go further than this; every book with play value is tested to the highest standards – if it fails, it's back to the drawing-board.

Made Fairly
We are working to ensure that the workers involved in our supply chain – the people that make our books – are treated with fairness and respect.

Responsible Forestry
We are committed to ensuring all our papers come from environmentally and socially responsible forest sources.

**For more information, please visit our website at
www.egmont.co.uk/ethical**